For Josh Hughes, who really knows about robots
—I.W.

For Martin
—A.R.

SAMMY
and the ROBOTS

by **Ian Whybrow**
illustrated by **Adrian Reynolds**

ORCHARD BOOKS • NEW YORK

It was a shock for Sammy
when his robot fell over.
It was just doing a nice march and
suddenly its lights went out.

Sammy heard Gran coughing in the yard, so he ran out to show her.

One of the robot's batteries had leaked onto its wires. Sammy and Gran packed up the robot and sent it to the robot hospital.

"They'll know how to fix it," Gran said.

Sammy wanted to make another robot to play with while he waited for his marching robot to come back.

"Good idea," said Gran. "We'll use my best scissors if you'd like."

They laid out everything they needed on the table.

But they never got started.
Gran's cough was so bad that
Mom made her go to bed.

When Sammy woke up the next morning,
there was no Gran.
"She had to go to the hospital because of her
cough," Mom explained.

Sammy started to make a robot all by himself.
He wanted to use Gran's best scissors, just like she had
said he could.

But Meg said, "No! Those are Gran's!"

That was why Sammy threw his stegosaurus at her.

Mom took him aside to settle down. She said,
"You may use Gran's best scissors if she said so,
but only while I'm watching."

Sammy worked hard all
morning . . .

. . . and before long there was a new robot.
Sammy taught it to march.
He taught it to talk.
But best of all he taught it to blast.
The robot said,
  "Ha-lo-Sam-mee.
  Have-you-got-a-cough?
  BLAAAST!"

BLAAAST!

The hospital was big, but they soon found Gran.

Mom said Meg and Sammy had to wait outside Gran's room. They waved through the window, but Gran did not open her eyes.

Meg and Mom whispered with the doctor.
So Sammy slipped into the room with his new
robot.

He held the robot close to Gran.
The robot said,
"Ha-lo-Gran.
Do-you-have-a-cough?"
Gran opened one eye. It winked.
The robot said,
"I-will-blast-your-cough.
BLAAAST!"

Mom ran in. "Sammy! No!" she cried.
But the doctor said not to worry. A robot would be a
good helper for Gran.

That evening Sammy was very busy.

He joined . . .

he stuck . . .

he painted . . .

and soon he had made
five more robots
for Gran.

They guarded her. They marched
for her. And they blasted her cough.
In no time at all, she was better.

Gran came home and unpacked her things.
"You're a good looker-afterer," she whispered.
"And my robots?" said Sammy.
"Oh yes, those too," said Gran. "I'd like to keep them with me, if you don't mind."
Sammy did not mind at all.

Gran went out into the yard to check on
the chickens. They were just fine.

That afternoon a package arrived. It was the marching robot, back from the robot hospital. Its light glowed, and it did a nice march—good as new.